Mothers

A mother is a female parent. Mothers have children.

At Home

Nina's mom makes breakfast before she goes to work.

MY ENGINEER

Ty's mom reads to him
at bedtime.

Eddie's mom mows the lawn.

Work and Play

Alice's mom teaches piano lessons.

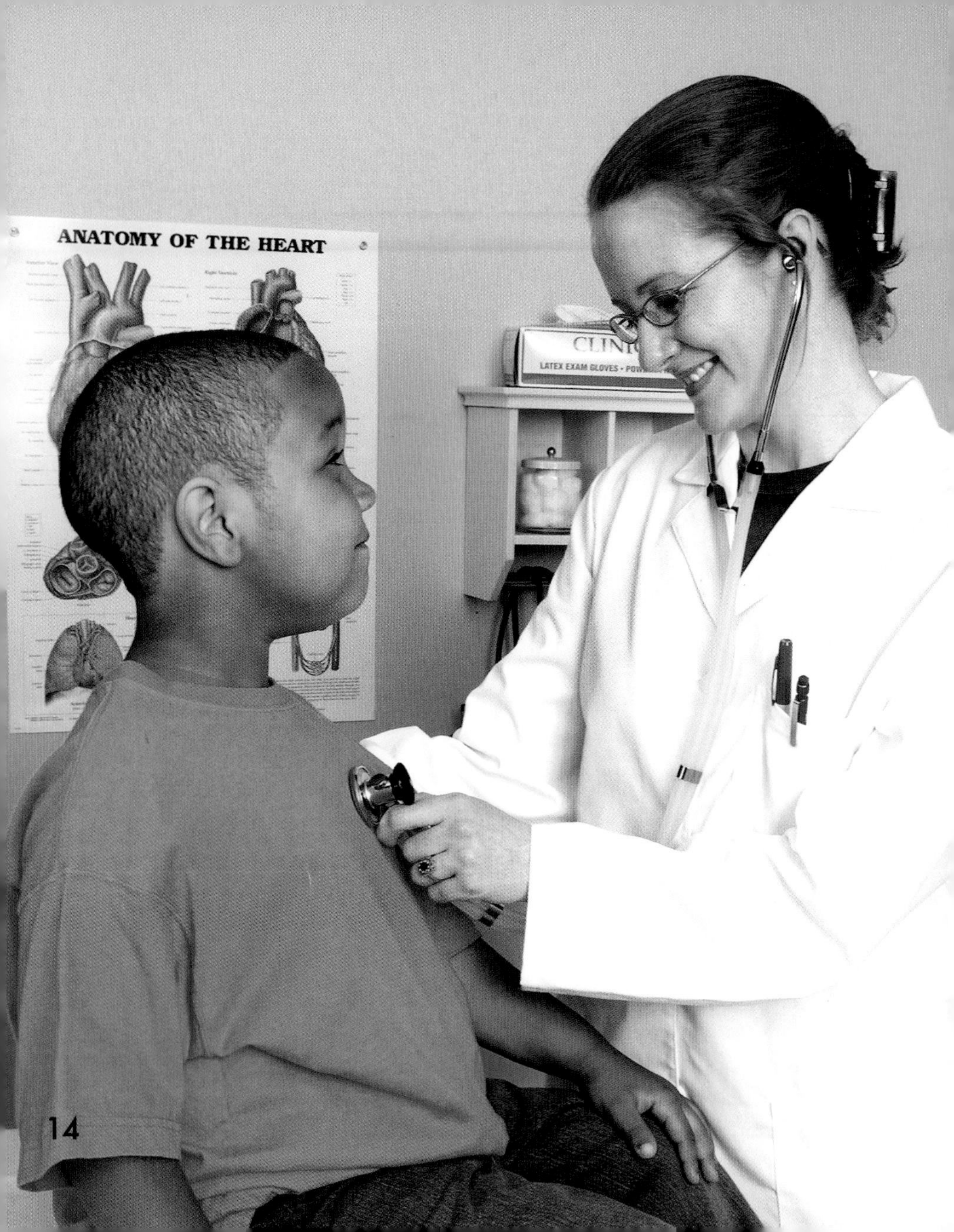
ANATOMY OF THE HEART
LATEX EXAM GLOVES

Al's mom is a doctor.

30

Andy's mom watches football.

Grace's mom golfs.

Mothers love.

Glossary

lesson — a set time for teaching a certain skill

mow — to cut grass; mothers do many chores inside and outside.

parent — a mother or a father of one child or many children; when a parent has more than one child, the children are called siblings.

teach — to show someone how to do something new

Read More

Easterling, Lisa. *Families.* Our Global Community. Chicago: Heinemann, 2007.

Sirett, Dawn. *Mommy Loves Me.* New York: DK, 2006.

Internet Sites

FactHound offers a safe, fun way to find Internet sites related to this book. All of the sites on FactHound have been researched by our staff.

Here's how:

1. Visit *www.facthound.com*
2. Choose your grade level.
3. Type in this book ID **1429612274** for age-appropriate sites. You may also browse subjects by clicking on letters, or by clicking on pictures and words.
4. Click on the **Fetch It** button.

WWW.FACTHOUND.COM

FactHound will fetch the best sites for you!

Index

Word Count: 49
Grade 1
Early-Intervention Level: 10

Editorial Credits
Sarah L. Schuette, revised edition editor; Kim Brown, revised edition designer

Photo Credits
Capstone Press/Karon Dubke, all